Mendel's Accordion

HEIDI SMITH HYDE

illustrations by
JOHANNA VAN DER STERRE

KAR-BEN
PUBLISHING

For Martin, Andrew and Steven —H.S.H.

To my father, Kees van der Sterre, who loves music —J.v.d.S.

Kar-Ben Publishing, Inc.
A division of Lerner Publishing Group
241 First Avenue North
Minneapolis, MN 55401 U.S.A.
1-800-4KARBEN

Website address: www.karben.com

Library of Congress Cataloging-in-Publication Data

Hyde, Heidi Smith.
    Mendel's accordion : the story of the klezmorim / by Heidi Smith Hyde ;
illustrations by Johanna van der Sterre.
        p.   cm.
    ISBN-13: 978—1—58013—212—1 (lib. bdg. : alk. paper)
    ISBN-10: 1—58013—212—X (lib. bdg. : alk. paper)
    1. Klezmer music—History and criticism—Juvenile literature.
2. Accordion—Juvenile literature.   I. Sterre, Johanna van der.   II. Title.
ML3528.8.H93 2007
781.62'924—dc22   2005036002

Manufactured in the United States of America
1 2 3 4 5 6 — DP — 12 11 10 09 08 07

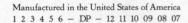

MENDEL LIVED in a small village called
Melnitze. He didn't have much. A hut . . . a
cow . . . a rooster . . . some hens . . . and
an accordion.

It wasn't a fancy accordion. Nothing about Mendel was fancy. It had worn, black buttons up and down the sides for Mendel's busy fingers, and big folds in the middle like a lady's fan. Mendel pumped those folds with his strong arms, pushing the air in and out, in and out, turning it into music.

Mendel made beautiful music with that accordion. Everywhere he went, people said, "Play for us, Mendel!" And Mendel did.

HE WENT from town to town, village to village. Others joined him along the way. Soon, Mendel found himself in a band. Yankele played the fiddle. Herschel played the clarinet. Hymie played the drums. Zalman played the flute. And Shmelke played the cello.

Together, they were known as the "klezmorim."

The klezmorim never stayed in one place for too long. They went from town to town, village to village. Everywhere they went, people said, "Play for us, klezmorim!" And they did.

They played at weddings and festivals and fairs.
They played happy music. They played sad music.
People laughed. People cried. The village was
alive with the sounds of the klezmorim.

THEN ONE DAY, people stopped laughing. Life was hard in the village, and there was never enough food. It was so hard that Mendel decided to leave Melnitze.

He sold his hut. He sold his cow. He sold his rooster. He sold his hens.

Mendel boarded a boat for America, taking only his accordion with him.

On the boat, Mendel met other klezmorim. There was Mottel from Moscow, Itzik from Odessa, and Pinchus from Pinsk. Mottel played the clarinet, Itzik played the violin, and Pinchus played the flute. "Soon we will be in America," they said. "Soon we will be in the Golden Land!"

GOLDENE MEDINA

But the boat ride seemed to last forever, and two weeks seemed like two years as the boat rose and fell and the cold winds blew.

"Come, let us do something," said Mendel as the passengers groaned and grumbled along with the boat. He couldn't bear to see everyone so unhappy.

And so Mendel from Melnitze played his accordion.
Mottel from Moscow played his clarinet.
Itzik from Odessa played his violin.
And Pinchus from Pinsk played his flute.

Though their stomachs churned, they played and played and played some more. They played happy music. They played sad music. People laughed. People cried. The boat was alive with the sounds of the klezmorim.

It was like being back home in Melnitze.

FINALLY, THEY reached America and Mendel and his
new friends boarded a ferry for New York. They were tired
and cold, and their bodies ached from the long journey.

"It's crowded here," remarked Pinchus when they
arrived in New York. "I've never seen so many people!"
Clutching his accordion, Mendel had to agree.
There were no rolling hills or peaceful farmhouses
or wandering chickens. Just rows and rows of brick
buildings, and lots and lots of people who spoke a
different language.

"Don't worry," said Mendel. "We will all find jobs and a place to live. America will be good to us, you'll see!"

"Mendel is right," agreed Itzik. "We will all find good jobs and a place to live."

And so they did.

Mendel found a job mending shoes.
Mottel and Pinchus worked in a rope factory, and Itzik
played his violin in a minstrel show.

They all lived together on the Lower East Side of
New York.

Mendel worked long hours.
The city was big. The apartment was small.
But Mendel was happy.
He had good friends and a good job and a place to live.

Soon he had a wife, too! Her name was Reizel, and
like Mendel, she was from the old country.

Reizel loved listening to Mendel's accordion.
Sometimes after a long day at work, he would
serenade her in the kitchen.

He played happy music. He played sad music.
Reizel laughed. Reizel cried. The little apartment
was alive with the sounds of the klezmorim.

As the years passed, Mendel's accordion continued to delight his growing family. His son Isaac loved singing along with the music. His son Aaron loved to dance wildly in the middle of the room. And baby Rose just sat on her mother's lap and listened quietly to the funny Yiddish words.

During the day, there was work but at night there was music. Always music! Sometimes Mottel, Itzik, and Pinchus came over and played together just like the old days.

It was like being back home in Melnitze.

YEARS PASSED, and before Mendel knew it, his children had grown up. Just like Mendel, they loved music, only a different kind of music. Mendel's son Isaac liked jazz. His granddaughter Rachel played swing, and his great-grandson Samuel loved rock-and-roll.

Nobody listened to Mendel's accordion anymore.

Melnitze was but a distant memory.

THEN ONE DAY, Samuel was rummaging around in the attic when he made a wonderful discovery: a dusty, old accordion with worn, black buttons up and down the sides and big folds in the middle like a lady's fan.

It was so dusty and old that it needed to be repaired. The man at the music shop said it probably hadn't been played in more than 50 years. It was a wonder he got it to work at all.

Samuel had heard stories of his great-grandfather Mendel and his remarkable klezmorim.

"I'm going to learn to play this accordion," he told his family. "I'm going to learn to play just like Mendel!"

And so Samuel practiced and practiced and practiced some more. Soon he found himself in a band.

Leon played the fiddle.
Barry played the clarinet.
Steven played the drums.
Ellen played the flute.
And Andrew played the cello.

Together they were known as the "New Klezmorim."
Everywhere they went, people said, "Play for us, klezmorim!"
And they did.

They played at weddings and anniversaries. They played
happy music. They played sad music. People laughed.
People cried. But mostly they smiled.

The New World was alive with the sounds of the klezmorim.